AN UGLYDOLL™ COMIC

EAT DAT!

KIM | HORVATH | NICHOLS | JACOBSON | MCGINTY | COOPER | LEDBETTER

EAT DAT!

AN UGLYDOLL COMIC

COVER ART: SUN-MIN KIM AND DAVID HORVATH
COVER AND BOOK DESIGN: FAWN LAU
EDITOR: TRACI N. TODD

Printed in China

Published by VIZ Media, LLC
P.O. Box 77010
San Francisco, CA 94107

10 9 8 7 6 5 4 3 2 1
First printing, January 2014

End papers by Sun-Min Kim and David Horvath | **"Food Fight"** story by Travis Nichols, art by Ian McGinty, colors by Michael E. Wiggam | **"No Share"** part 1 story and art by Sun-Min Kim and David Horvath | **"Taste Buds"** story by Travis Nichols, art by Phillip Jacobson, colors by Michael E. Wiggam | **"Samplin'"** story by Travis Nichols, art by Ian McGinty, colors by Michael E. Wiggam | **"Treeberry Pie"** story and art by Dave Cooper | **"Flavorville"** story by Travis Nichols, art by Phillip Jacobson, colors by Michael E. Wiggam | **"No Share"** part 2 story and art by Sun-Min Kim and David Horvath | **"Babo's Bakery"** story by Travis Nichols, art by Ian McGinty, colors by Michael E. Wiggam | **"Delicious"** story and art by Joe Ledbetter | **"Mover and Little Bent's Lunch on the Gooooo"** story and art by Travis Nichols | **"Don't Overdo It"** story and art by Sun-Min Kim and David Horvath | **"Hot in the Shade"** story by Travis Nichols, art by Phillip Jacobson, colors by Michael E. Wiggam | **"Sweet Victory"** story by Travis Nichols, art by Phillip Jacobson, colors by Michael E. Wiggam | **"Black Belt Juice Ninjanator"** story and art by Travis Nichols | **"Stone Soup"** story by Travis Nichols, art by Ian McGinty, colors by Michael E. Wiggam | **"Back in the Ugly Day"** story and art by Sun-Min Kim and David Horvath

TABLE OF CONTENTS

WHO

BABO

WEDGEHEAD

NINJA
BATTY
SHOGUN

MYNUS

ICE-BAT

TRAY

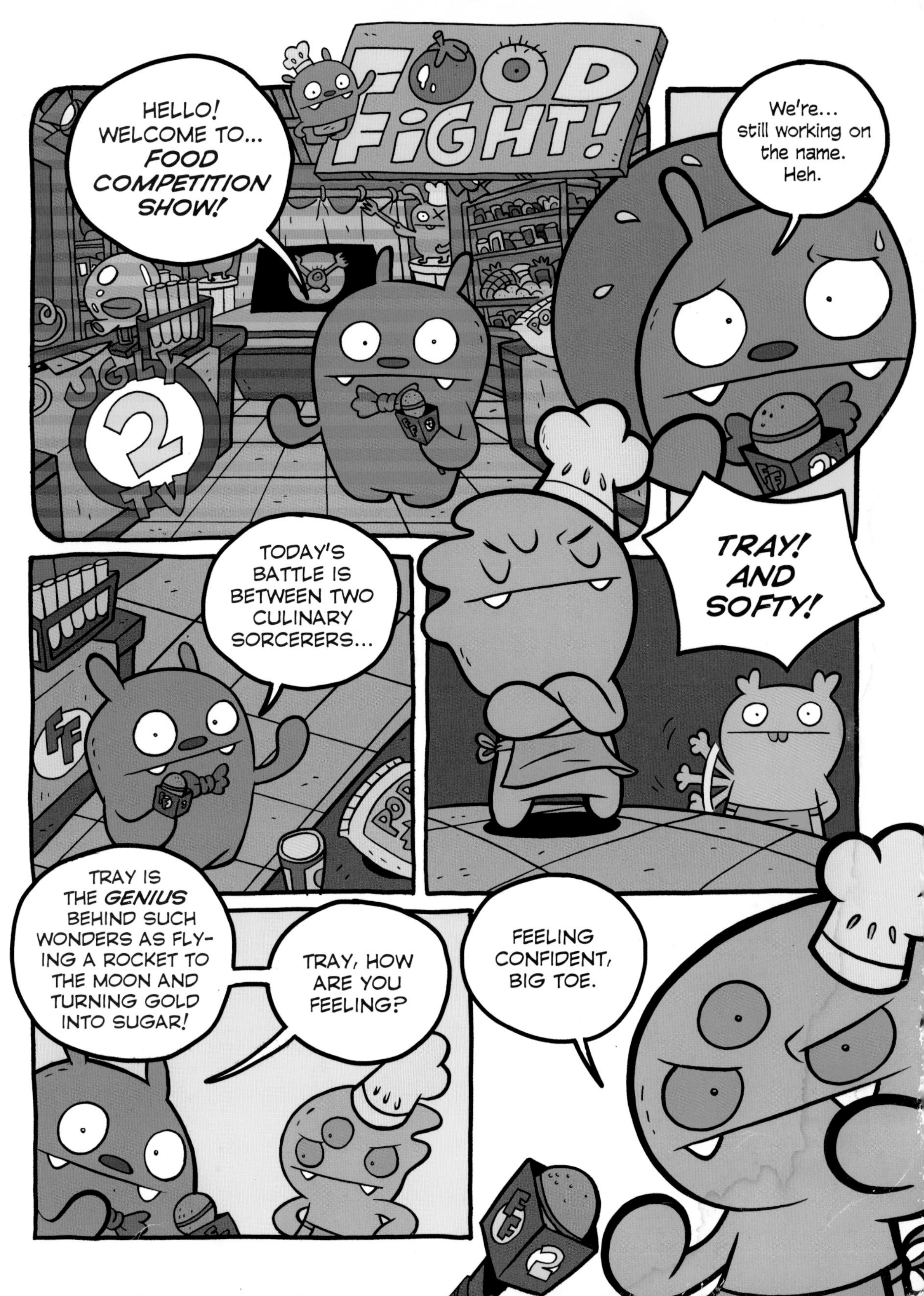
FOOD FIGHT!
HELLO! WELCOME TO... FOOD COMPETITION SHOW!
We're... still working on the name. Heh.
TODAY'S BATTLE IS BETWEEN TWO CULINARY SORCERERS...
TRAY! AND SOFTY!
TRAY IS THE GENIUS BEHIND SUCH WONDERS AS FLY-ING A ROCKET TO THE MOON AND TURNING GOLD INTO SUGAR!
TRAY, HOW ARE YOU FEELING?
FEELING CONFIDENT, BIG TOE.

SOFTY! YOU'VE RECENTLY MASTERED COUNTING TO SIX!
WELL, I DON'T KNOW ABOUT *MASTERED*, BIG TOE!
ALRIGHTY THEN. LET'S DO THIS! ***TO YOUR STATIONS!***
THREE... TWO...ONE... ***MAKE FOOD!***
MAWS
CORN
FF
I'M PREPARING A FEAST FOR ALL *EIGHT* SENSES. IT'S ONE PART CHEMISTRY, ONE PART GASTRONOMY AND ONE PART ASTROLOGY. SHIELD YOUR EYES.
FWOOOSH!

HOW EXCITING TO SEE SCIENCE IN THE KITCHEN!
SOFTY... WHAT'RE YOU UP TO OVER HERE?
CORN
CRACK!
I'M MAKING MY SPECIAL BREAK-AND-TEAR SALAD.
I...I'M NOT ALLOWED TO USE KNIVES. Or ovens.
RIP!
I WISH WE'D HAD THAT INFORMATION EARLIER.
WELL...MAY THE BEST UGLY WIN!

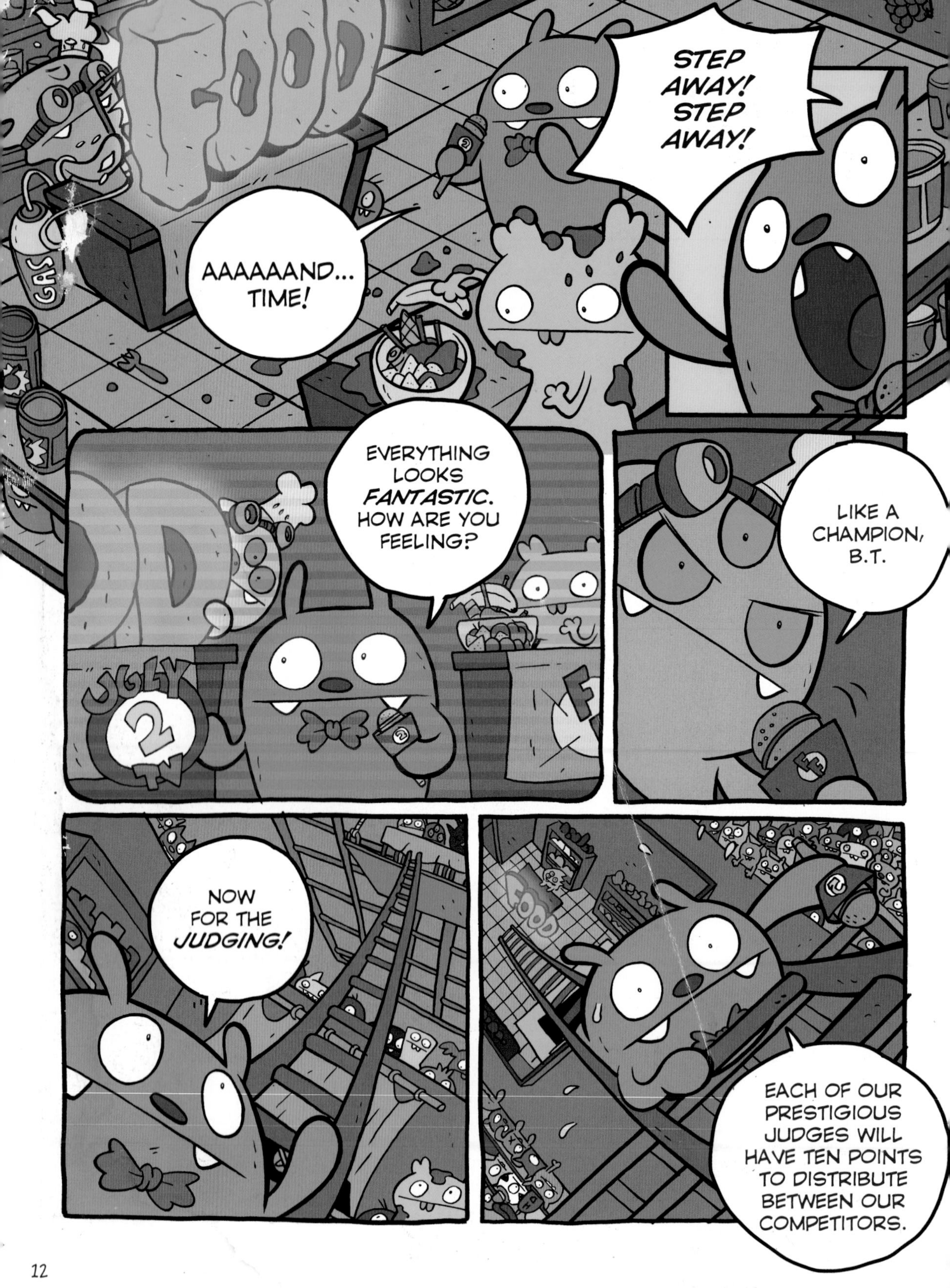
FOOD
STEP AWAY! STEP AWAY!
GAS
AAAAAAND... TIME!
EVERYTHING LOOKS *FANTASTIC*. HOW ARE YOU FEELING?
UGLY 2 TV
LIKE A CHAMPION, B.T.
NOW FOR THE *JUDGING!*
FOOD
EACH OF OUR PRESTIGIOUS JUDGES WILL HAVE TEN POINTS TO DISTRIBUTE BETWEEN OUR COMPETITORS.

WHEW!
THIS TABLE IS WAY TOO HIGH. I MEAN... GASP! I GET WANTING TO BE DRAMATIC, BUT STILL.
OKAY! TO OUR JUDGES!
HE'S GHOSTY! TAKE IT AWAY, GHOST-AAAY!
UGLY 2 TV
CHEW CHEW CHEW!
GULP
MMHMM. MMHMM...
!
PLOP!
PLOP!
WAAA! DON'T LOOK AT ME! DON'T LOOK AT ME!
YUM SHOW
UTV

Should we just keep going? I don't... OKAY! JUDGE NUMBER TWO!
HE'S FRIENDLY! HE'S AN OVER-ACHIEVER! HE'S A VISION IN A BLUE APRON!
UGLY 2 TV
HE'S *WAGE! LET'S HEAR IT!*
THEY'RE BOTH WONDERFUL. SUCH GOOD FRIENDS.
5
5
I GIVE FIVE POINTS TO TRAY...
...AND FIVE POINTS TO SOFTY!
!
5
WE HAVE A TIE! A TIE!

EVERYTHING HINGES ON THE DECISION OF OUR THIRD AND FINAL JUDGE.
UGLY 2 TV
HE'S LIVELY! HE'S WILD! HE'S... A BIT OF A TROUBLE-MAKER!
HE'S GASSY! (AND HE HASN'T EVEN TRIED THE FOOD...)
Very funny. WELL, BIG T. TASTE ISN'T EVERYTHING. THE REAL TEST IS HOW WELL THIS STICKS TO THE WALL!
BOOM SHAKA LAKA!
SMASH!
PING
[INSERT NAME OF SHOW HERE] CHAMPION

NO NO NO
NO NO NO
NO NO
NO NO NO!
OOPS.
WELL, I GUESS THAT'S THE END OF OUR SHOW... RIGHT AFTER WE DECLARE...
THE WINNERS!!
THE END

To be continued...

TASTE BUDS

THE NOGGIN SCRAMBLER BOASTS THE LARGEST LOOP- DE-LOOP IN ROLLER-COASTER HISTORY!

OOH. LOOPS.

CRUNCH
CRUNCH

THIS IS ALSO GOOD TOO AS WELL.
WAIT. FLIP OVER.

FLIP
CRUNCH
CRUNCH

FORSOOTH, THE LIGHT SPRINKLING OF CINNAMON IS THE PERFECT COMPLIMENT TO A NUTTY, OATY CRUNCH.

AND SO...

UNTIL FINALLY...

UPSIDE DOWNLICIOUS
CULINARY COMMENTARY BY WEDGINALD J. HEAD

SALE
THIS IS IT, WEDGINALD. WE'RE GONNA BE WICH!
WHAT?
STUFF
SALE?

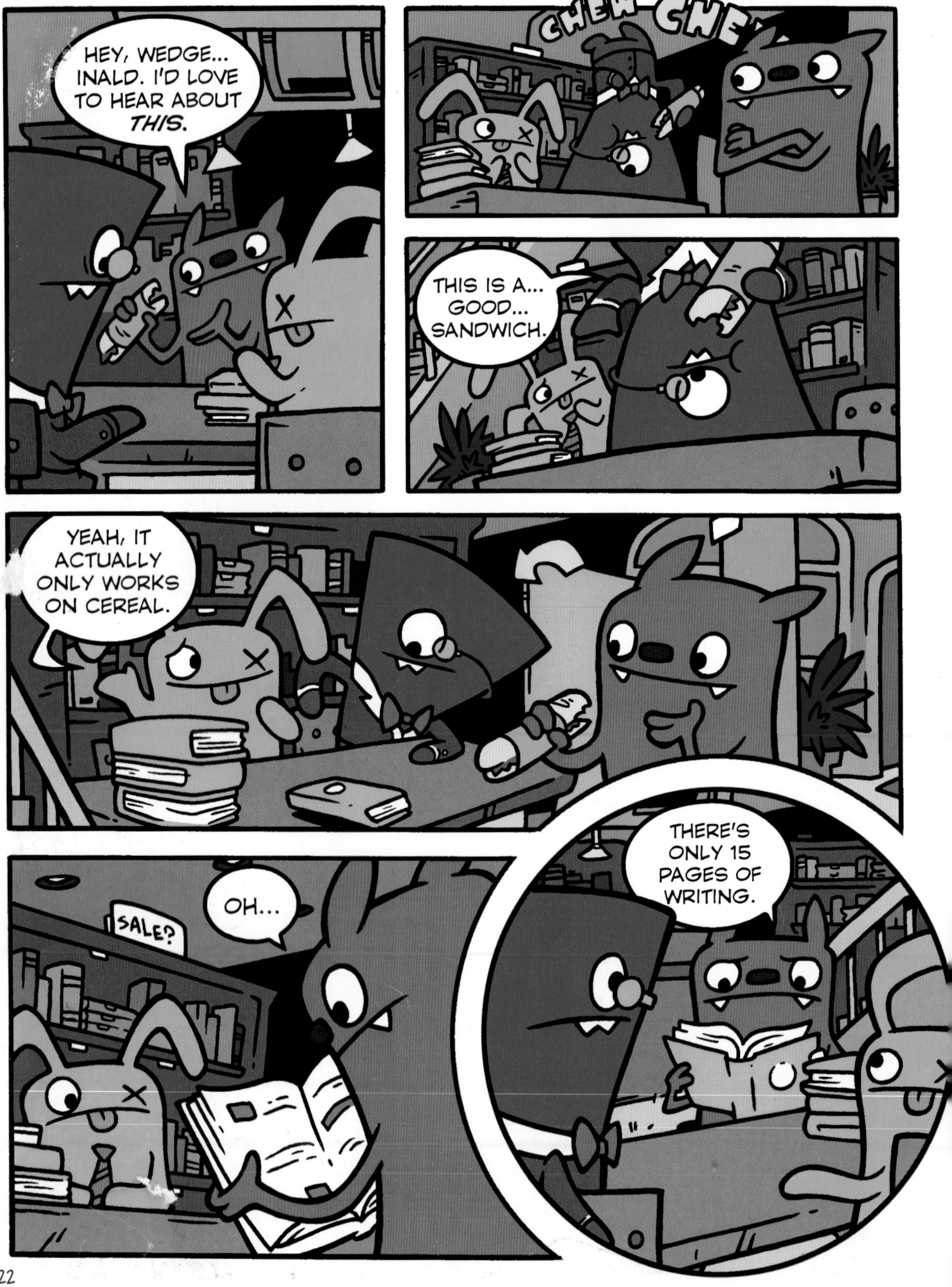

YEAH, IT ACTUALLY ONLY WORKS ON CEREAL.

SALE?

OH...

THERE'S ONLY 15 PAGES OF WRITING.

THAT...IS AMAZING.

SIR, I'M GOING TO HAVE TO ASK YOU TO PAY FOR THAT.

YIKES!

GUESS AGAIN.

SAMPLIN'
TEENY TACOS
FREE SAMPLES! TRY A TEENY TACO™ TODAY!
COOL.
YEP. LOOKS ABOUT RIGHT.
WHY, THANK YOU, MY GOOD MAN. CHEERIO!

WELL, SHUCKS! LIL' OL' TACOS!

MUCH OBLIGED, TENDERFOOT.

TRICK OR TACO!

YAR! TACO OFF THE STARBOARD BOW!

HELLO. I AM WEDGEHEAD.

WHOOOOOOA! GNARLY TACOS, BRAH!

Shuffle
Shuffle

NAB!

WHAT YEAR IS IT? ARE THERE STILL TACOS? *ARE THERE?*

YOU HAVE JUST SAVED THE GALAXY!

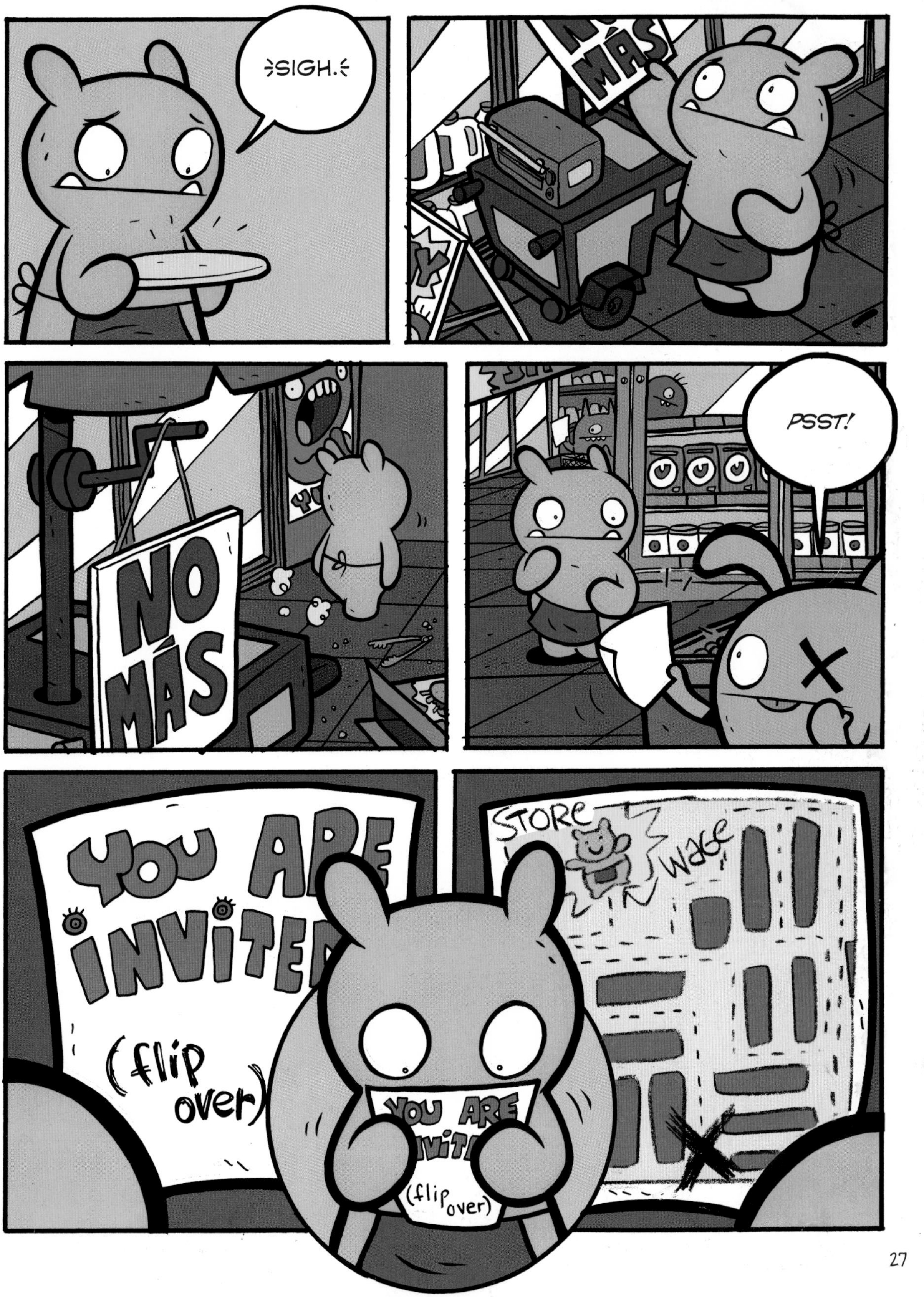

YOU ARE

(flip over)

STORE

wage

FROZEN FOOD
2
3
OOKIES
$2
FRO ZEN SOCKS
JUST SAUSAGES!
A TON O' BEAN

FLOWERS

FAKE FLOWERS
NOT REAL!

IRREGULAR
NO GOOD ...
MAYBE ...
SPORT
SPORTS
SMALL
BIG

BASEBALL CARDS
JELLY
BIKE TIRES
BABY BIRDS
CHIPS
PEAS
BOOKS
PILES OF STUFF
SAND
OUTDOOR FURNITURE
HOME GOODS
RUITS
WELCOME!

DINNER IS SERVED!
I...I DON'T KNOW WHAT TO SAY, OX. *THANK YOU!*
I'M SO HAPPY YOU LIKED IT. AND NOW, YOUR BILL.
WILL THAT BE CASH OR CHARGE?
PLOP!
end!

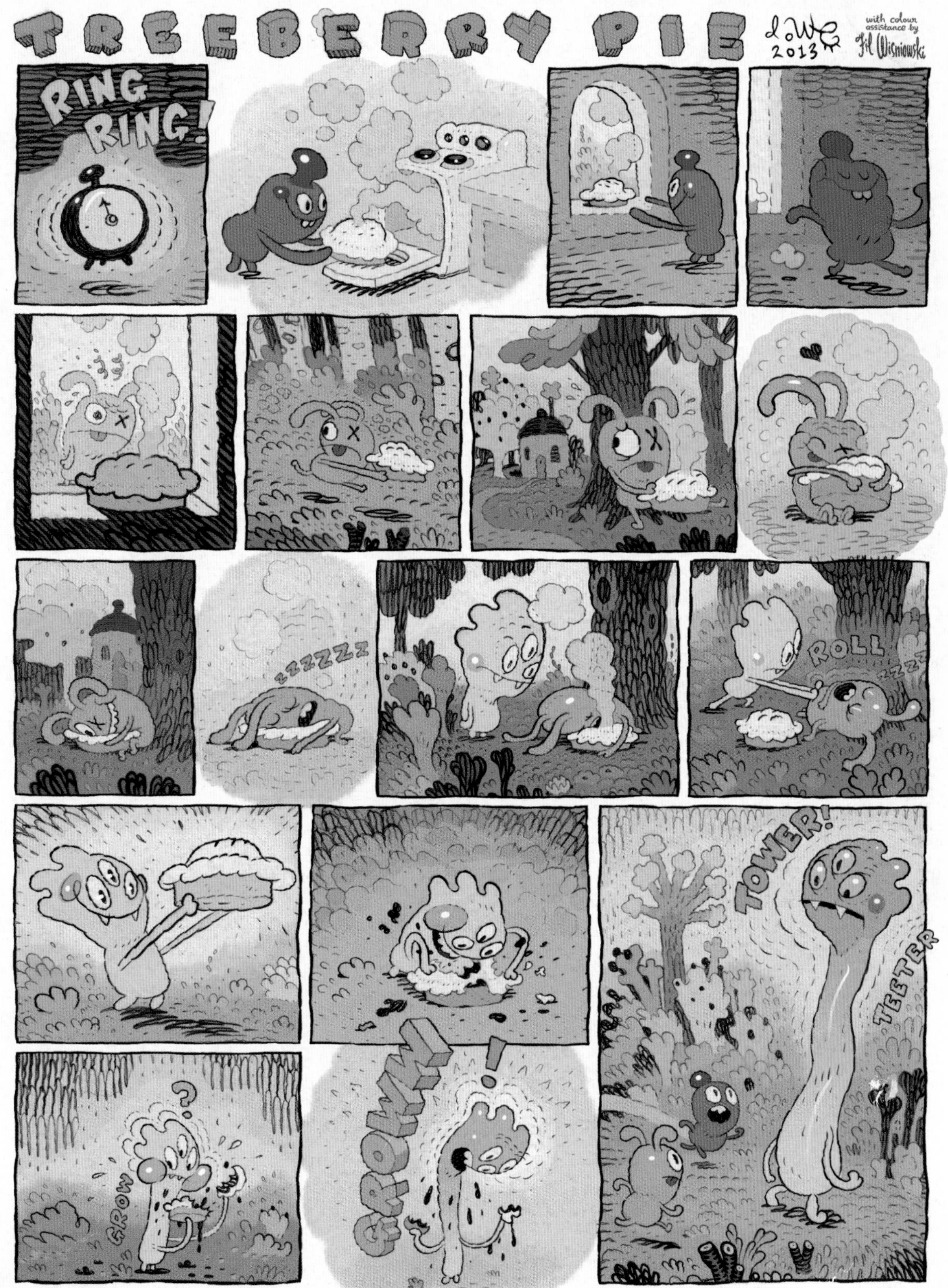
TREEBERRY PIE
2013
with colour assistance by
Fil Wisniowski
RING RING!
ZZZZZZ
ROLL
ZZZZ
?
GROW
GROW
!
TOWER!
TEETER

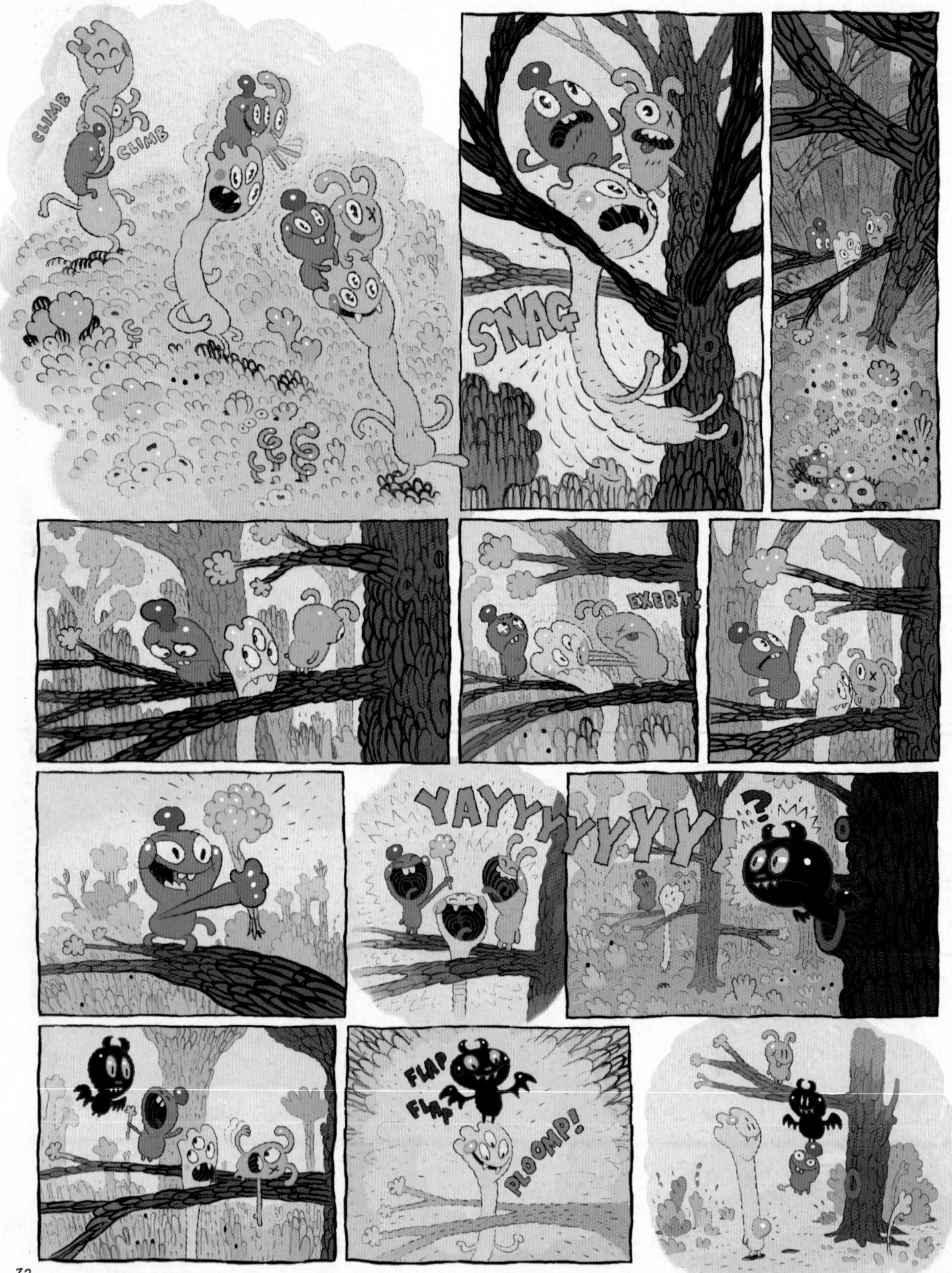

CLIMB
CLIMB
SNAG
EXERT!
YAYYYYYYYY!
?
FLAP
FLAP
PLOOMP!

THE BEGINNING

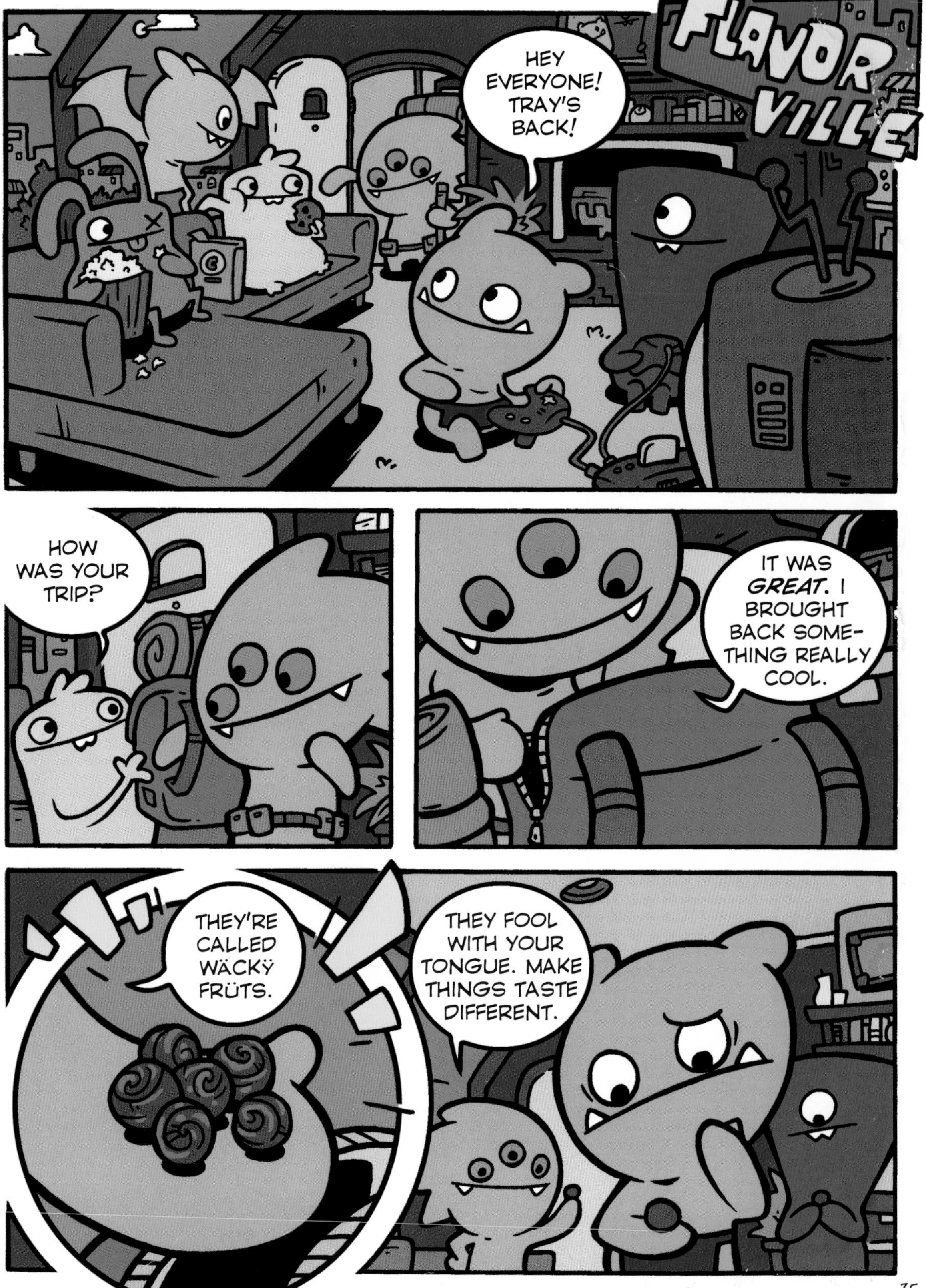

FLAVOR VILLE

HEY EVERYONE! TRAY'S BACK!

CHEW
CHEW
CHEW

MY TONGUE IS TINGLING.
COOK

WHOA!

YOURS TOO, ICE-BAT!

OKAY! LET'S EAT!

TASTES LIKE A HUBCAP!

DO-NUT
CALL 65225
LOST
FOUND
HERE GOES...
ENCHI-
LADAS!
FOUND
WHAT
THE?!

SALT-
WATER
TAFFY?
WOW!

WOO!
CAREFUL, GUYS.
THIS WINDOW
IS SPICY.

OOH!
GUACAMOLE!
BIG
BOY

OOH!
THAT'D
GO GREAT
WITH THESE
TORTILLA
CHIPS!

TRAY!
OVER
HERE!
BLUE-
BERRY
PIE!
YOU'RE
WELCOME.

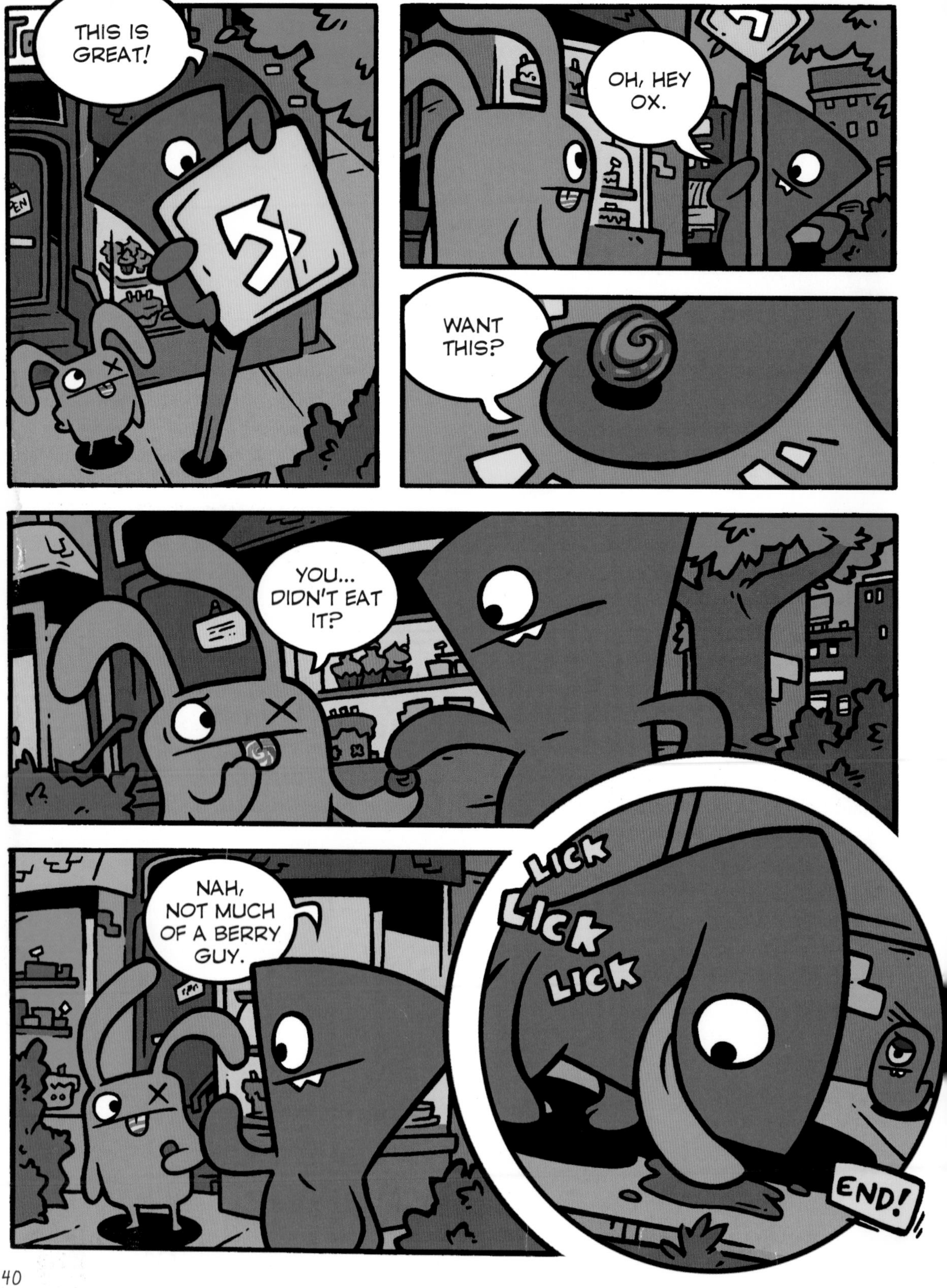

YOU... DIDN'T EAT IT?

NAH, NOT MUCH OF A BERRY GUY.

LICK
LICK
LICK

END!

NO SHARE PART 2

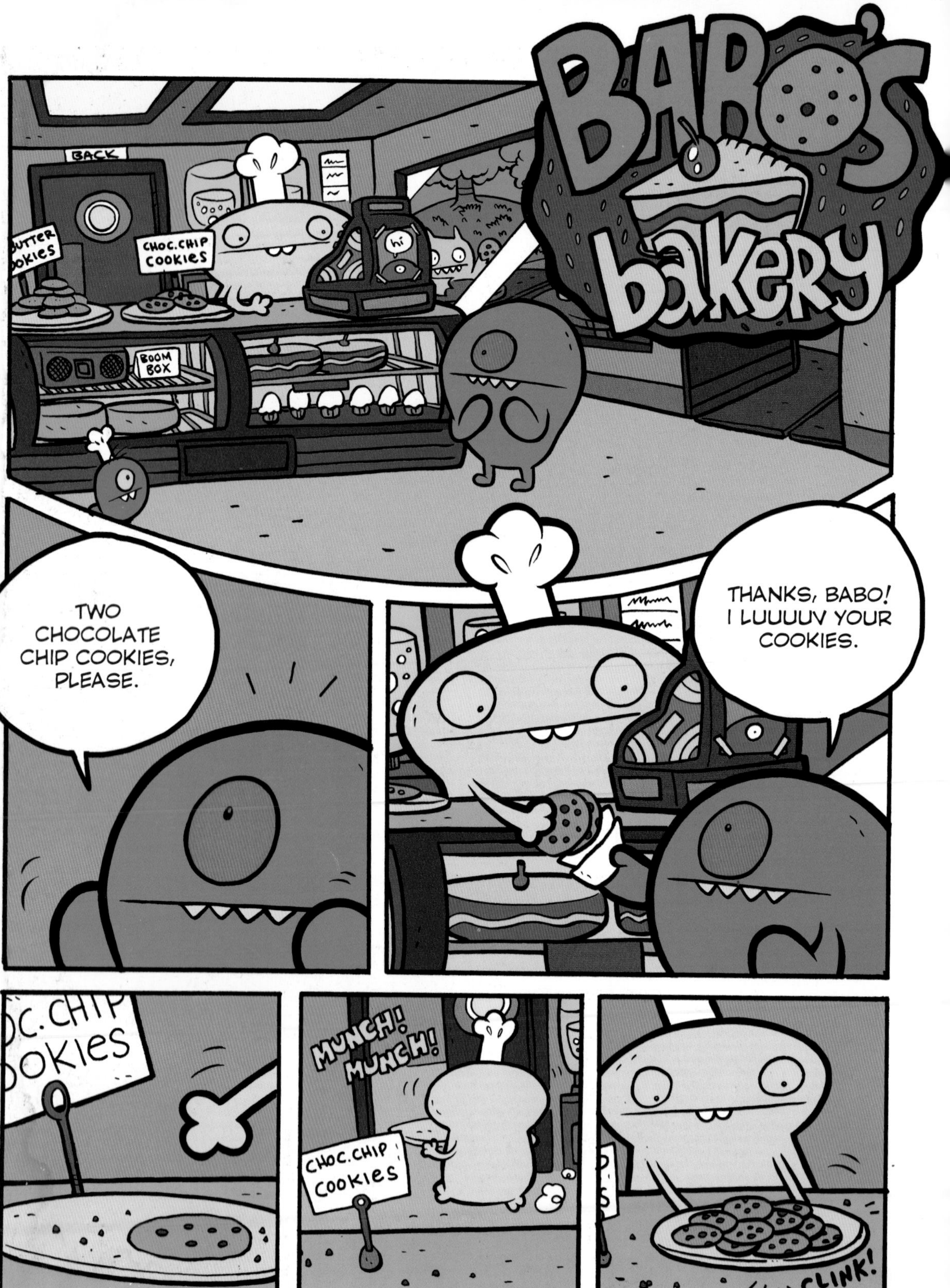

BABO'S bakery

BACK

UTTER
OKIES

CHOC. CHIP
COOKIES

hi

BOOM
BOX

TWO CHOCOLATE CHIP COOKIES, PLEASE.

THANKS, BABO! I LUUUUV YOUR COOKIES.

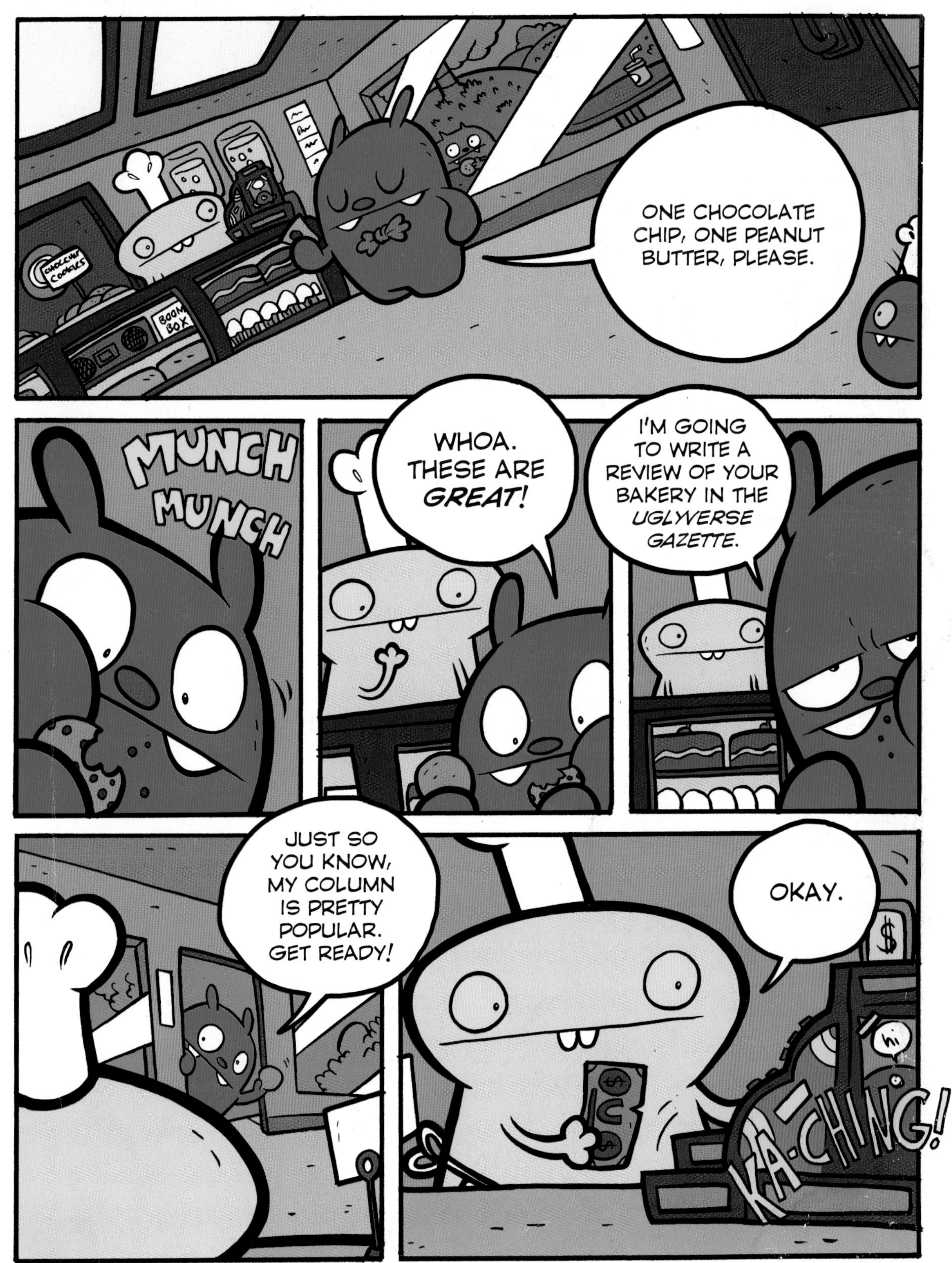
CHOCOLATE COOKIES
BOOM BOX
ONE CHOCOLATE CHIP, ONE PEANUT BUTTER, PLEASE.
MUNCH MUNCH
WHOA. THESE ARE *GREAT*!
I'M GOING TO WRITE A REVIEW OF YOUR BAKERY IN THE *UGLYVERSE GAZETTE*.
JUST SO YOU KNOW, MY COLUMN IS PRETTY POPULAR. GET READY!
OKAY.
hi
KA-CHING!

THE NEXT DAY
BABO'S
BABO'S
CHOC CHIP COOKIES
ONE PEANUT BUTTER COOKIE, BAKERDUDE.
hi
BOOM BOX
CHIP COOKIES
OH NO, OH NO. IS HE OUT? ARE THEY SOLD OUT?
WHEW!
CLINK!
BOOM BOX

YEAH, YEAH. LISTEN. HOLD ON. I'M AT A PLACE.

HEY. YEAH. ONE OF THOSE THINGS.

STLL THERE? INNOVATION IDEATION DOWNSIZING—HOLD ON.

KID, THESE ARE FANTASTIC.
BOX

HOW WOULD YOU LIKE TO SELL YOUR COOKIES AT *UGLYMART?*

OKAY.
COOK DUDE!
WAIT—

WE'LL NEED A HUGE KITCHEN! LOTS OF BAKERS! BOXES! LABELS! WITH ANY LUCK WE'LL BE UP-AND-RUNNING IN A FEW MONTHS!
FROSTBITE WUZ HERE
BABO'S
BABO'S
ROLL! ROLL! ROLL!
HAVE YOU SEEN ME?
I AM UGLY!
Beep!! Beep!
BABO'S
CHOCOLATE CHIP
BABO'S
ICED GINGERBREAD
BABO'S
PEANUT BUTTER
CELERY
HMM... SIGN HERE.

SOON...
DESTROY ALL OBSTACLES
LIVE
UGLYMART
POP!
BABO! LISTEN. WE'RE GOING TO NEED TO QUADRUPLE OUR ORDER!
CHOC. CHIP COOKIES
OKAY.
AND A COUPLE MORE VARIETIES?
LIVE
BABO'S
BABO'S
OKAY.
HOW DOES HE *DO* IT?!
ADMINISTRATIVE ASSISTANT! BRING ME SOMETHING SHINY AND EXPENSIVE THAT I'LL GET BORED WITH ALMOST IMMEDIATELY!
BEEP!

MUSH
PIZZA
CARROT
ROUND FRUITS!
YO!
FOOD
BABO'S
CHOCOLATE COOKIE
HEE HEE HEE! SHINY!
BABO'S
ZIP!
SIGH.
BABO'S
BABO'S
RRUMM!
BABO'S
VROOOM!!

A DOZEN BLACK-AND-WHITE COOKIES.
NO! WE AGREED ON 12!

THERE HE IS!
2765
DON'T EAT THE FLOUR

BABO! YOUR COOKIES ARE THE BEST EVER! THEY'RE THE HOTTEST THINGS ON THE *PLANET!*
2765

TELL US: HOW DO YOU DO IT?!
UGLY 2 TV

OKAY.
UGLY 2 TV

2765
THIS IS IT, FOLKS. THE SCOOP OF THE CENTURY!

BOX
GASP!

END!
SQUAAAAAWK!
SQUAAAAAWK!
SQUAAAAAWK!
SQUAAAAAWK!
SQUAAAAAWK!
SQUAAAAAWK!
SQUAAAAAWK!

Delicious
BY JOE LEDBETTER
YOU LOOK DELICIOUS.
NO, YOU LOOK DELICIOUS.
YOU'RE BOTH DELICIOUS.
CHOMP!!
HEY FIRE-CAT, DID YOU SEE MY LUNCH?
I DID! IT WAS DELICIOUS! WHATCHA GONNA DO ABOUT IT?
THAT'S THE LAST STRAW, FIRE-CAT! AN ICE-BAT CAN ONLY TAKE SO MUCH!
J.LED

FLWAPP!
SWEET. THAT SHOULD HOLD HIM FOR A BIT.
NOW, WHAT TO DO ABOUT LUNCH.
GRRRRR
SPLACK
mmmmmmm... DELICIOUS!
HELP
ME TOO!
J.LED

SNAP
YAY!
UFF...
WHOA
THANKS, FIRE-CAT. YOU SAVED ME!
WHO ELSE AM I GOING TO STEAL MY LUNCH FROM? BESIDES, YOUR COOKING IS DELISH!
YOU KNOW, JUST 'CAUSE I'M AN ICE-BAT AND YOU'RE A FIRE-CAT DOESN'T MEAN WE CAN'T BE FRIENDS.
WHY DON'T WE JUST EAT LUNCH TOGETHER?
BUDDIES?
PALS!
UHH... SO WHO'S BUYING?
END!
J.LED

Are you like us? Always on the move, making it loathsome, nay, IMPOSSIBLE to stop for lunch?

Frankly, just standing here and talking is driving me NUTS.

TRAVIS NICHOLS '13

Oh yeah. WRAP. As in lunch wraps.

Right. So tell them what they need.

Hold on. I'm at the bottom of the ocean studying seaweed.

Okay. I'm back. They need food. And wraps.

Yeah yeah. Then put the food in the wrap and go.

OKAYBYE

DON'T OVER DO IT!

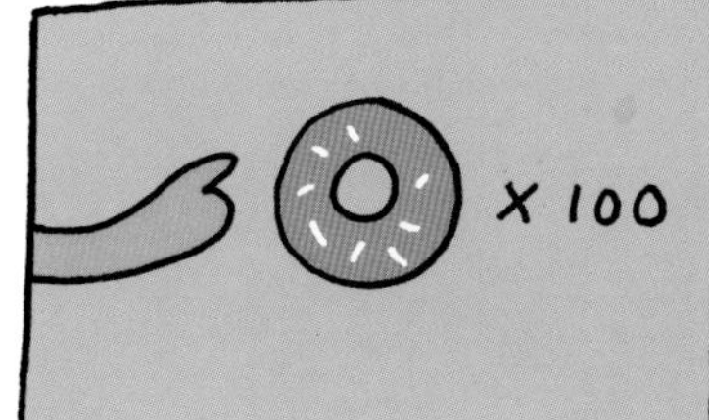

HOT IN THE SHADE

BLAAAA AAAAAAA AAAH...

SUGAR!
SUGAR

WATER!

LEMONS!

LET'S DO THIS.
幸せ

IT'S NOT... RIGHT.

MORE SUGAR?

NO, THAT'S NOT IT... Sure is hot out here...

MORE LEMONS?

HMM... NOPE. MORE WATER?

NOW IT'S...NOT SWEET ENOUGH? I DON'T KNOW.

POUR

TOO SWEET!
SUGAR!

TOO SOUR!
PAF

HERE. LET'S USE THIS.

THAT'S NOT IT!

WISH WE COULD FIGURE THIS OUT!

I REALLY... JUST... DON'T...

WHEW!
SURE IS HOT!
OOH!
LEMONADE?

NEEDS
MORE
LEMONS.

SEE,
THAT'S WHAT
I THOUGHT,
BUT I DON'T
KNOW.
OKAY,
DRAG IT
OVER
HERE!

THIS
SHOULD
DO IT!
I HOPE
SO! I'M
MELTING!

MORE... LEMONS?

HEY EVERYBODY!

WHAT'S GOING ON?
THAT'S IT!

FINALLY!
END

SWEET VICTORY
CUPPA
HEY, JEERO! WANT A BITE OF MY PANCAKES? THEY'RE SOOO GOOOOOOD.

YAAAAAA

TRAY:
BREAKFAST 2MORROW?
NO!

TKA TKA TKA TKA
JEERO:
WHAT WOULD WE BE HAVING?

"THE USUAL. HASH-BROWNS, PANC—"

FWIP

LATER...

WHAT'S GOING ON, BUDDY?

I CAN'T... IT'S TOO PAINFUL.

IT'S OKAY, JEERO. WE'RE YOUR PALS. YOU CAN TELL US ANYTHING.

WELL...IT WAS A BEAUTIFUL DAY IN THE PARK...
FLAPJACK THROWDOWN!
HOUSE of LEAVES
SIGN UP HERE!

I THOUGHT, "WHY NOT? I WORK OUT!"
FLAP-JACK THROWDOWN
JEERO

I ATE AND ATE...
5

...AND ATE AND ATE.
FINALIST
HOUSE of LEAVES
5

IN THE END, I WAS SO FULL... I COULDN'T MOVE. IT HURT.
SYRUP

OH, THE PAIN!
1:23

WELL...
I JUST...
NEVER
AGAIN.

HEY, ALL!
I GOT KICKED
OUT OF THE
PIZZA PLACE,
SO I GOT
WAFFLES.

GO-GO
WAFFLES!!

YUM!!

GO-GO
WAFFLES!

END!

TRAVIS NICHOLS

UGSN
BLACK BELT JUICE NINJA NATOR
₩29.99
500/500
0:28:52
Simply load the Chamber of Ultimate Vigor.

UGSN
BLACK BELT JUICE NINJA NATOR
₩29.99
500/500
0:28:47
Folks, this included recipe is full of vitamin-rich vegetables, whole grains...

UGSN
BLACK BELT JUICE NINJA NATOR
₩29.99
500/500
0:28:44
...quasi-legal nutrient powder blends...

UGSN
BLACK BELT JUICE NINJA NATOR
₩29.99
500/500
0:28:40
And pineapple for a little extra sweetness!

UGSN
BLACK BELT JUICE NINJA NATOR
₩29.99
500/500
0:28:32
Now, the patent-pending Ninjatronic 22-blade system in the Ninjanator can Blenderize™ ANYTHING.
BBJN
TM

UGSN
BLACK BELT JUICE NINJA NATOR
₩29.99
500/500
0:28:23
FOLKS, THE NINJANATOR IS NOW LIQUIDINATING™ THESE INGREDIENTS BETTER THAN ANY BLENDER IN THE HISTORY OF HOME APPLIANCES!!!
RRRRRRRR

UGSN
BLACK BELT JUICE NINJA NATOR
₩29.99
498/500
0:28:14
Ninja Batty Shogun will now show you how this simple, delicious, three-gallon juice can give your body an entire week's worth of nutrition.
RRP!

UGSN
BLACK BELT JUICE NINJA NATOR
₩29.99
498/500
0:28:08

UGSN
BLACK BELT JUICE NINJA NATOR
₩29.99
498/500
0:28:01
DOWN THE HATCH!

UGSN
BLACK BELT JUICE NINJA NATOR
₩29.99
498/500
0:27:53
Mmmmmmffggrrr!!!!

UGSN
BLACK BELT JUICE NINJA NATOR
₩29.99
498/500
0:27:49
G-g-g-gulp!

UGSN
BLACK BELT JUICE NINJA NATOR
₩29.99
498/500
0:27:45
Ooh... This is bad.

UGSN
BLACK BELT JUICE NINJA NATOR
₩29.99
498/500
0:27:43
OUTTATHEWAY!

UGSN
BLACK BELT JUICE NINJA NATOR
₩29.99
498/500
0:27:42
CRASH!
THE CAMERA! WATCH OUT!

UGSN
BLACK BELT JUICE NINJA NATOR
₩29.99
498/500
0:27:38
BLEEEAGH! BLARG! FFFFT!

UGSN
BLACK BELT JUICE NINJA NATOR
₩29.99
498/500
0:27:35
UUUUGGG....
CAMERA TWO! CAMERA TWO!

UGSN
BLACK BELT JUICE NINJA NATOR
₩29.99
114/500
0:27:31
Folks, let me assure you that this product—

UGSN
BLACK BELT JUICE NINJA NATOR
₩29.99
SOLD OUT!
0:27:29
Oh. We... we sold out. Wow. Thanks for watching.

and so...
UGSN
OBLITERIZINATOR
₩39.99
498/498
0:30:00
Hi, folks! Jeero and Big Toe here with the must-have gadget for every home.
LITERIZ-NATOR

UGSN
OBLITERIZINATOR
₩39.99
498/498
0:29:51
What if I told you that this one item could eliminate every problem in your LIFE?

UGSN
OBLITERIZINATOR
₩39.99
498/498
0:29:46
Bad grade on a book report?
JEERO G-
"A tale of Two Uglies"
It was the best of... Thither...

UGSN
OBLITERIZINATOR
₩39.99
498/498
0:29:44
Mountain of dirty dishes in the sink?

UGSN
OBLITERIZINATOR
₩39.99
497/498
0:29:41
Rusted-out car in the driveway?

UGSN
OBLITERIZINATOR
₩39.99
497/498
0:29:38
OBLITERIZINATE IT!
END!

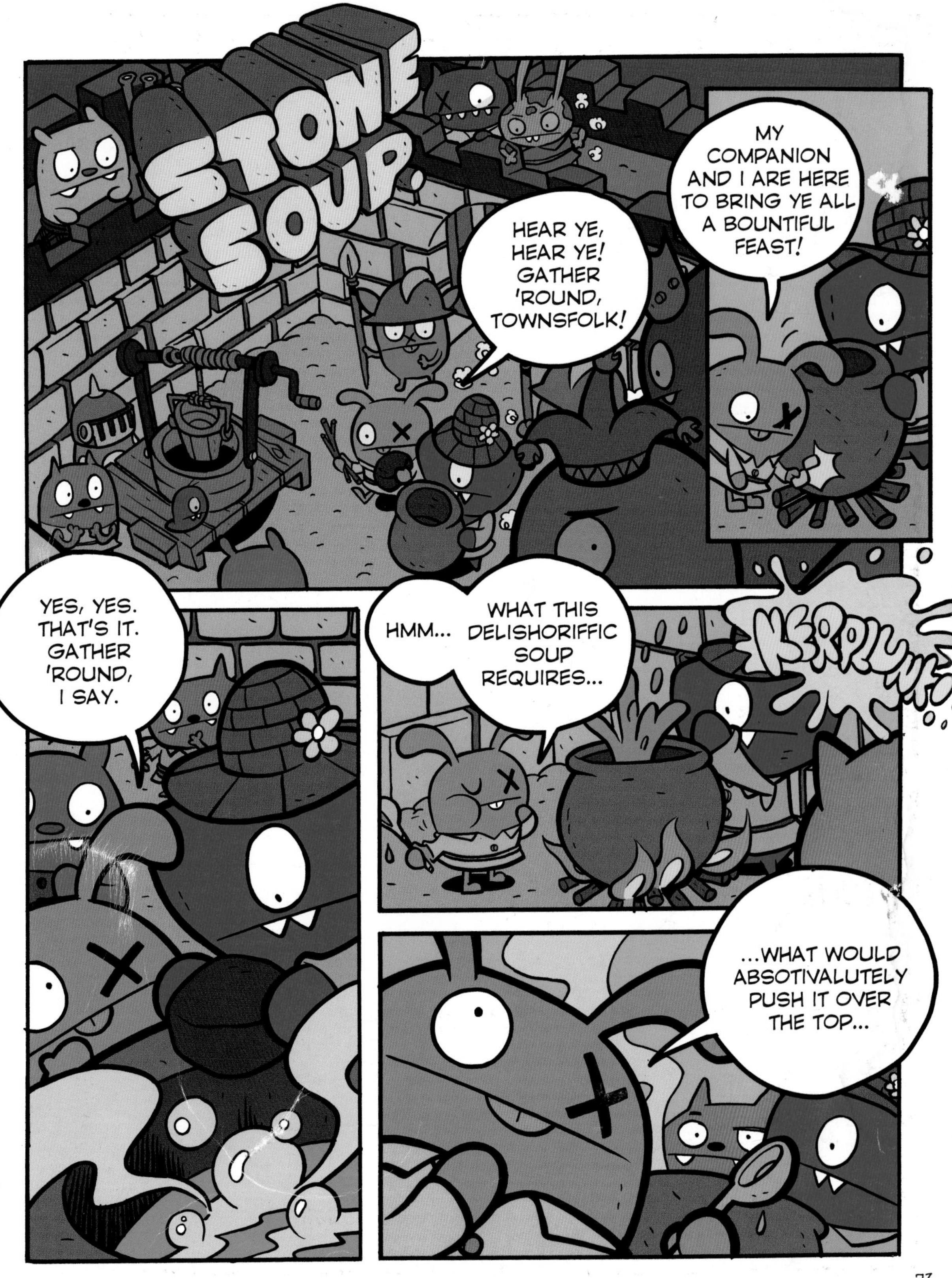
STONE SOUP
HEAR YE, HEAR YE! GATHER 'ROUND, TOWNSFOLK!
MY COMPANION AND I ARE HERE TO BRING YE ALL A BOUNTIFUL FEAST!
YES, YES. THAT'S IT. GATHER 'ROUND, I SAY.
HMM...
WHAT THIS DELISHORIFFIC SOUP REQUIRES...
KERPLUNK!
...WHAT WOULD ABSOTIVALUTELY PUSH IT OVER THE TOP...

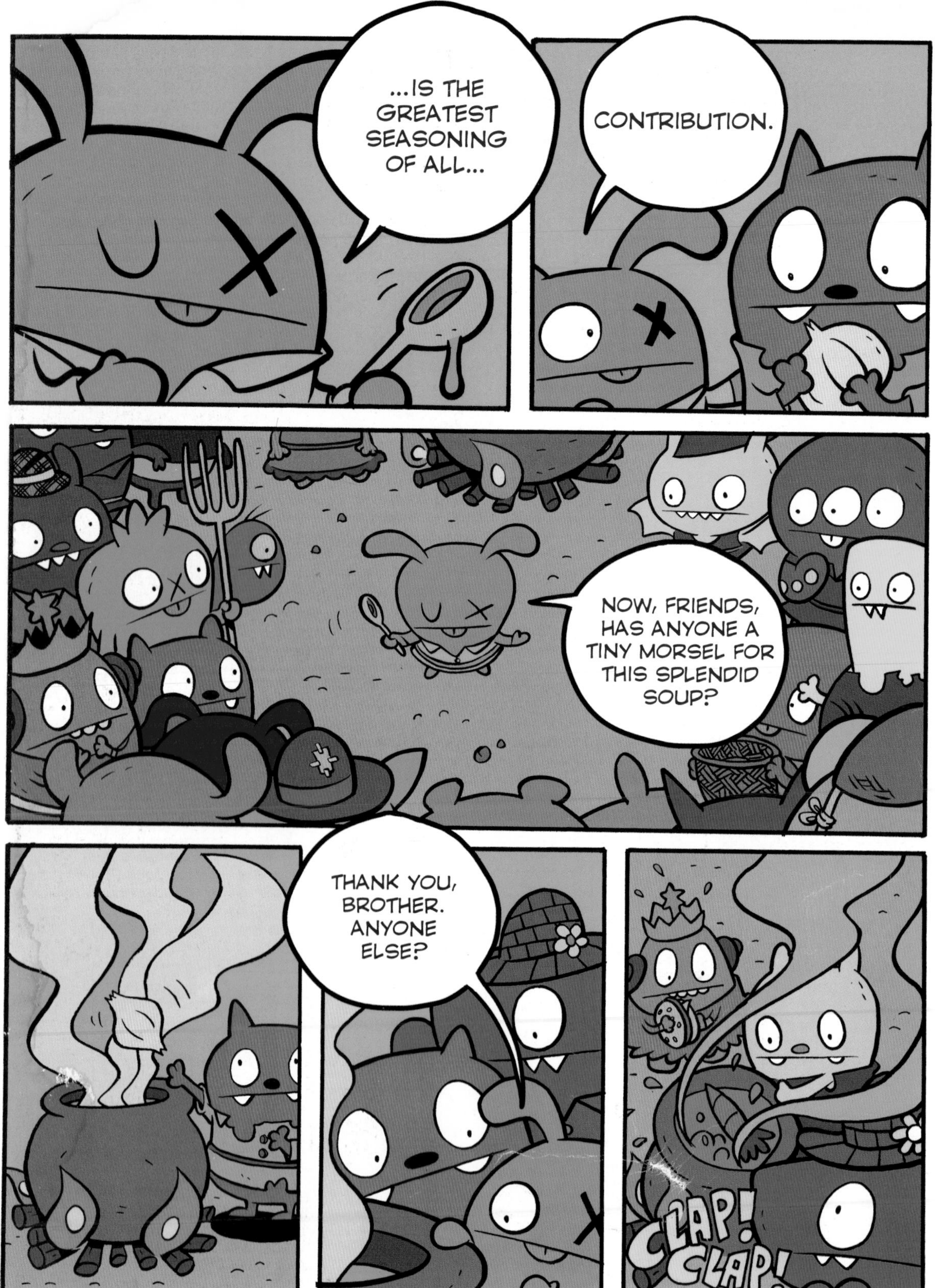
...IS THE GREATEST SEASONING OF ALL...
CONTRIBUTION.
NOW, FRIENDS, HAS ANYONE A TINY MORSEL FOR THIS SPLENDID SOUP?
THANK YOU, BROTHER. ANYONE ELSE?
CLAP! CLAP!

I'M BUFF
PROTEIN POWDA
WOW
POP!

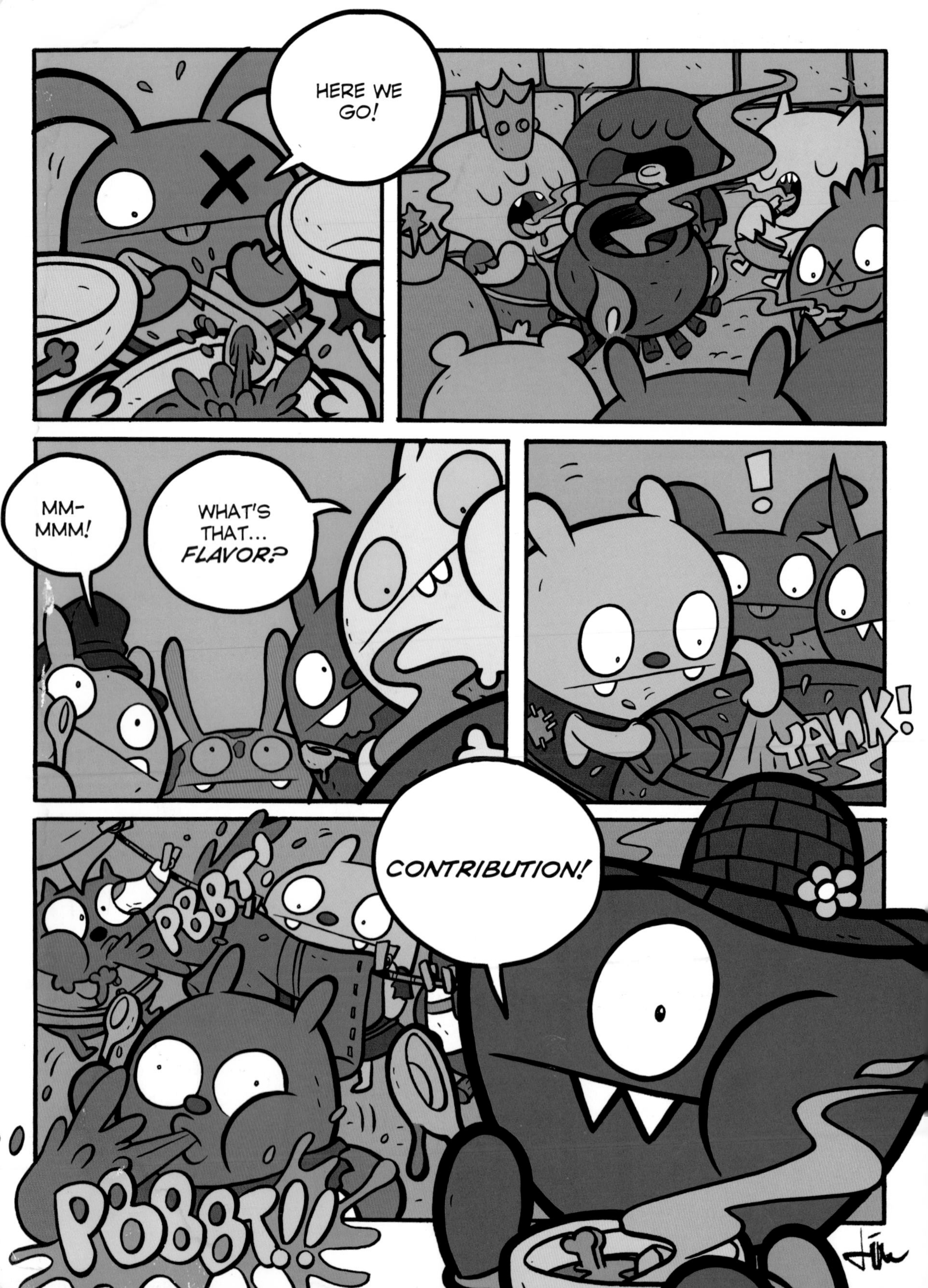
HERE WE GO!
MM-MMM!
WHAT'S THAT... FLAVOR?
!
YANK!
PBBT
CONTRIBUTION!
PBBBT!!

BACK IN THE UGLY DAY

Sun Min DAVID

BROUGHT

SUN-MIN KIM & DAVID HORVATH

are best known for creating the world of Uglydoll, which started as a line of handmade plush dolls and has since grown into a brand loved by all ages around the world. Their works can be found everywhere from the Moma in Tokyo and the Louvre in Paris, to the windows of their very own Uglydoll shop in Seoul. Sun-Min and David's very first conversation was about the meaning of "ugly." To them, ugly means unique and different, that which makes us who we are. It should never be hidden, but shouted from the rooftops! They wanted to build a world that showed the twists and turns that make us who we are, inside and out, because the whole world benefits when we embrace our true, twisty-turny selves. So, ugly is the new beauty. This Uglydoll comic features some of Sun-Min and David's heroes from the pop art and comic art world.

TRAVIS NICHOLS

is the author and illustrator of several books for kids and post-kids, including *The Monster Doodle Book*, *Punk Rock Etiquette* and *Matthew Meets the Man*. He previously drew comics for the late, great *Nickelodeon Magazine*. His deepest, most secret wish is to wake up as a gnome and spend his days building wooden locks, eating tiny biscuits and hanging out with birds. He can be found eating watermelon over the sink or online.

IAN MCGINTY

is a real smiley dude! And he wants to know where you got that cool lunchbox! You know, the one with the dinosaur riding a great white shark?
Oh, is this Gilbert Johnson? No? Gosh, sorry for bothering you! Um...okay, bye.

TO YOU BY:

PHILLIP JACOBSON

is a graduate of the Savannah College of Art and Design sequential art program. His earlier works include the self-published titles *Battle Mammals* and *Pancakes for Yeti*. Some of his influences include Bryan Lee O'Malley, Madeline Rupert and Craig Bartlett. He would like to thank his late grandmother Mary Ann Hill for constantly encouraging him to draw when he was little and for inspiring him to pursue his artistic goals.

DAVE COOPER

is a comic book guy, a gallery painting guy, a kid's book guy, and an aspiring television guy. He likes making up stuff, doesn't really matter what for.

JOE LEDBETTER's

distinctive style is deeply influenced by classic animation, underground comics, skateboarding and 1980s' video games. Over the years, Ledbetter has created an incredible cast of creatures to personify the human condition. With crisp bold lines and a vibrant palette, he mixes irony, social criticism and mischief, making his work universal and unmistakable.
Ledbetter is best known for his innovative and distinctive designer toys.

MICHAEL E. WIGGAM

is a professional comic book colorist whose work includes *Voltron Force* for VIZ Media, *Star Wars: Clone Wars* for Dark Horse Comics, Raymond E. Feist's *Magician Master: Enter the Great One* for Marvel Comics, R.P.M. and I.C.E. for 12 Gauge Comics, and various other publications. He was born and raised in Florida but has lived in Europe and seven U.S. states. Currently, he is earning an MFA from Savannah College of Art and Design.

FLT
THAT YOUR STOMACH?!
We've got just the thing.
Soup? Check. Tiny tacos? Check. Over-the-top high-stakes cooking competition? Check, check, check! But before you say, "Check, please!" treat yourself to a tour of Babo's Bakery, marvel at Wedgehead's culinary commentary and wash it all down with a chunky healthy shake. (Supplies are limited, so act now!) Yum!
Oh, and save room for a few tasty morsels from **Dave Cooper** and **Joe Ledbetter**!
COOKIES X 1000
Sorry we're OPEN
$7.99 USA $9.99 CAN £5.99 UK
ISBN-13: 978-1-4215-5724-3
50799
9 781421 557243
Sun Min + David
PERFECT SQUARE
viz media